When the Sorcerer goes out, leaving his magic hat behind, Mickey sees his chance to try his hand at some magic of his own. But things don't go as Mickey had planned.

First edition

WALT DISNEY'S
The Sorcerer's Apprentice

Ladybird Books Loughborough

There was once a great man who knew everything there was to know about magic.

He was called a sorcerer.

The sorcerer had a wonderful, tall, magic hat and whenever he wore his hat, he could just *think* magic.

He could think about a butterfly
and it would appear.

But only the sorcerer knew the
magic words to make it disappear.

The sorcerer did not live alone.
He had a helper named Mickey.
Mickey did all the work.

He swept the floor.

He chopped the wood.

He carried the water from the well.

Mickey knew about the magic of the hat.

"I wish I had that hat," said Mickey. "I would never have to work again. I would just *think* of what needed to be done and it would happen by magic!"

One day the sorcerer had to go out.
Mickey was alone at last
and there on the table
was the sorcerer's magic hat.

"Now I can be a great sorcerer,"
said Mickey.

He reached for the magic hat
and put it on his head.

An old broom was standing by the wall.

"I'll put a spell on that broom," said Mickey.

He did what the sorcerer always did. He thought magic thoughts and then pointed his fingers at the broom.

The broom began to move.

The broom grew feet.

It grew a right arm and then a left arm.

"Broom!"
commanded Mickey.
"Pick up the
buckets."
The broom did just
what Mickey said.

"Go up the steps,"
said Mickey. The broom
went up the steps.

"Fill the buckets
with water,"
said Mickey.

The broom filled the buckets.

"Bring them back," said Mickey.
The broom brought them back.

"Pour the water," said Mickey.
The broom poured the water.

Mickey danced around the room.

"Magic is easy," he cried.
"I will never have to work again."

Then Mickey sat down
in the sorcerer's chair.
"Work, broom, work!" he said.

While the broom went on filling
buckets and pouring water, Mickey
fell asleep. He dreamed he was the
greatest sorcerer in the world.

Suddenly something cold and wet woke him up. It was a splash of water.

Another splash knocked Mickey out of the chair.

Water was everywhere! The broom was flooding the room.

"Stop!" cried Mickey.

"Stop, broom! Stop, I say!"

But the broom did not stop
and Mickey didn't know the magic
words to make it stop.

Mickey pointed his finger at the broom but the broom kept going.

He held out his arms but the broom pushed him down.

He grabbed the bucket but the broom held on tight.

Wasn't there any way to stop the broom?

Mickey saw an axe
and he grabbed it.

He chopped the broom into bits.
"Well, that's the end of that
broom!"

But it wasn't the end.

Something strange was going on.

The bits of wood began to move.

The bits of wood turned into
brooms. All the new brooms had
feet and arms and buckets.

They marched up the steps and
they wouldn't stop.

The brooms came back with
more water.

Mickey leaned against the door to
keep them out but the brooms
pushed it open.

Mickey held out his arms to hold
them back but the brooms walked
right over him.

"I am a great sorcerer!" cried
Mickey. "You must do as I say."
But the brooms marched on
and on.

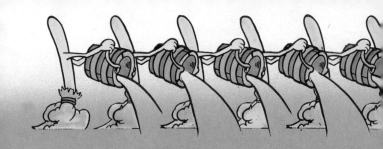

Brooms and more brooms!
Buckets and more buckets!
In a great line, they poured
and poured.

The water got deeper and deeper.
Poor Mickey! He could only just
keep his head above water.

Then the sorcerer's Book of Magic
floated by and Mickey grabbed it.

Page after page after page...
Mickey looked for the magic words
that would stop the brooms.

But the water began to whirl and
Mickey couldn't read the words.

He hung onto the book
as he went round
and round
and round in
the water.

Spinning faster
and faster,
Mickey was caught
in a great whirlpool.
Now there was nothing he could do.

Then a great dark shadow
appeared on the wall! The sorcerer
had come back.

He knew at once what Mickey
had done.

He raised his arms and roared a
great command. It was special
magic.

The brooms and the water
disappeared.

Only one broom was left and that
was the old broom, standing by the
wall.

The sorcerer was frowning.

He looked down at Mickey.

Then, with a mighty sweep of his
arm, he grabbed the hat from
Mickey's head.

"Just a little magic trick," said
Mickey and he tried to smile.

But the sorcerer did not smile.

The sorcerer looked down at his little helper. "Don't start what you can't finish," he said.

Mickey wondered if he would ever be a great sorcerer as he picked up the buckets and went back to work.

43